HILDEGARD
B1901
D1972

LORELEI
B1925
D1957

MELVIN
B1926

MILLY
B1929

SAM
B1944

ALICE
B1940

ROGER
B1945

RACHEL
B1945

CHARLIE
B1949

LUCY
B1950

KEVIN
B1942

LULU
B1951

CHI CHI
B1960

MEGAN
B1968

ANASTASIA
B1973

IAN
B1975

LENNY
B1975

SUE
B1972

MIKE
B1975

VAL
B1975

MORGAN
B1975

GWYNETH
B1973

JULIAN
B1969

FRAN
B1974

BARBARA
B2005

GINA
B1992

SIDNEY
B1998

SEAN
B1999

MAGGIE
B2000

STEVIE
B1997

KATHY
B1996

SARA
B1999

DAVE
B2000

LILI
B1995

GEORGE
B1997

DAISY
B1998

JAKE
B1999

CH
SEP 07

NOTE TO THE READER:

Cousins are often the most confusing part of family trees.

First cousins share the same grandparents,

second cousins share the same great-grandparents,

third cousins have the same great-great-grandparents, etc., etc.

If cousins don't have the same number of generations between them

and their common ancestor, they are "removed."

If there is a one-generation difference, the cousins are "once removed,"

if there is a two-generation difference, the cousins are "twice removed," and so forth.

G. P. PUTNAM'S SONS

A division of Penguin Young Readers Group. Published by The Penguin Group.

Penguin Group (USA) Inc., 375 Hudson Street, New York, NY 10014, U.S.A.

Penguin Group (Canada), 90 Eglinton Avenue East, Suite 700, Toronto, Ontario, Canada M4P 2Y3

(a division of Pearson Penguin Canada Inc.).

Penguin Books Ltd, 80 Strand, London WC2R 0RL, England.

Penguin Ireland, 25 St. Stephen's Green, Dublin 2, Ireland (a division of Penguin Books Ltd.).

Penguin Group (Australia), 250 Camberwell Road, Camberwell, Victoria 3124, Australia (a division of Pearson Australia Group Pty Ltd).

Penguin Books India Pvt Ltd, 11 Community Centre, Panchsheel Park, New Delhi - 110 017, India.

Penguin Group (NZ), Cnr Airborne and Rosedale Roads, Albany, Auckland 1310, New Zealand (a division of Pearson New Zealand Ltd).

Penguin Books (South Africa) (Pty) Ltd, 24 Sturdee Avenue, Rosebank, Johannesburg 2196, South Africa.

Penguin Books Ltd, Registered Offices: 80 Strand, London WC2R 0RL, England.

Published simultaneously in Canada. Manufactured in China by South China Printing Co. Ltd. Design by Gina DiMassi. Text set in Burghley Light.

Library of Congress Cataloging-in-Publication Data   Isadora, Rachel. What a family! | by Rachel Isadora.   p. cm.

Summary: Grandpa Max explains to Ollie the ways their relatives are connected.   [1. Family–Fiction. 2. Grandfathers–Fiction.]

I. Title. PZ7.I763Wh 2006 [E]–dc22 2004027543 ISBN 0-399-24254-6 10 9 8 7 6 5 4 3

WHAT A FAMILY!

A fresh look at family trees

by **RACHEL ISADORA**

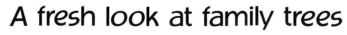

G. P. PUTNAM'S SONS   NEW YORK

OLLIE

Ollie is the shortest kid
in his kindergarten class.

Grandpa Max says Ollie looks just like his brother Winthrop did back in 1924 when he was the shortest kid in his kindergarten class.

OLLIE

GRANDPA MAX

WINTHROP

Ollie also looks like his brother Angelo,
who has hair that sticks straight up.

OLLIE

ANGELO

ROGER

Ollie and Angelo look like their first cousin once removed Roger, who has large ears that he can wiggle just like his granddaughter Sidney and his uncle Melvin.

Melvin's great-grandnephew Sean has big ears,
but can't wiggle them, and has blue eyes
just like his second cousins
Olivia, Louie, and
baby Barbara.

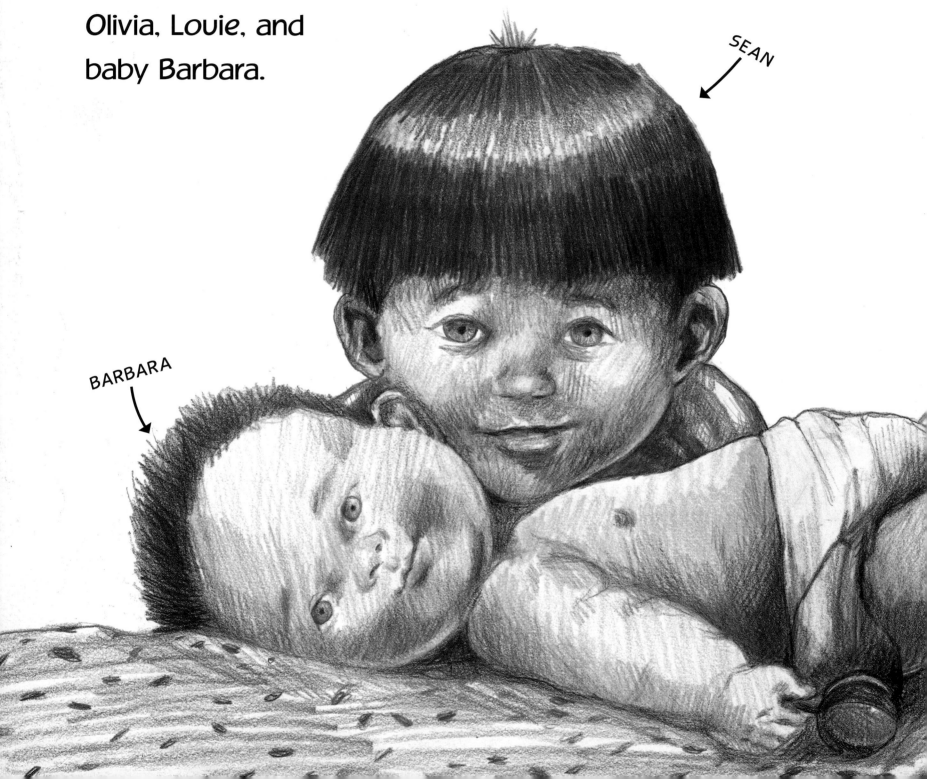

OLIVIA

LOUIE

Baby Barbara has red hair
like her third cousins
Lili and George.

GEORGE

Lili and George's twin second cousins once removed,
Kyla and Katie, have red hair, while their half sisters,

Talisha and Zinzi, have black hair like their father, Henry.

ZINZI

HENRY

JAKE

Henry's son, Mark, has dimples like his second cousin once removed Jake.

Jake wears glasses like his first cousins
once removed Lenny, Mike and Morgan
and their sons and daughters,
Stevie, Kathy, Sara and Dave.

Stevie, Kathy, Sara and Dave's second cousin
Daisy takes off her glasses when she sings
and holds a note longer than anyone.

Daisy's second cousin once removed Chi Chi
can hold a note a long time while
he plays his guitar left-handed.

Chi Chi's second cousin Jamela is left-handed and can bend her thumb back,

JAMELA

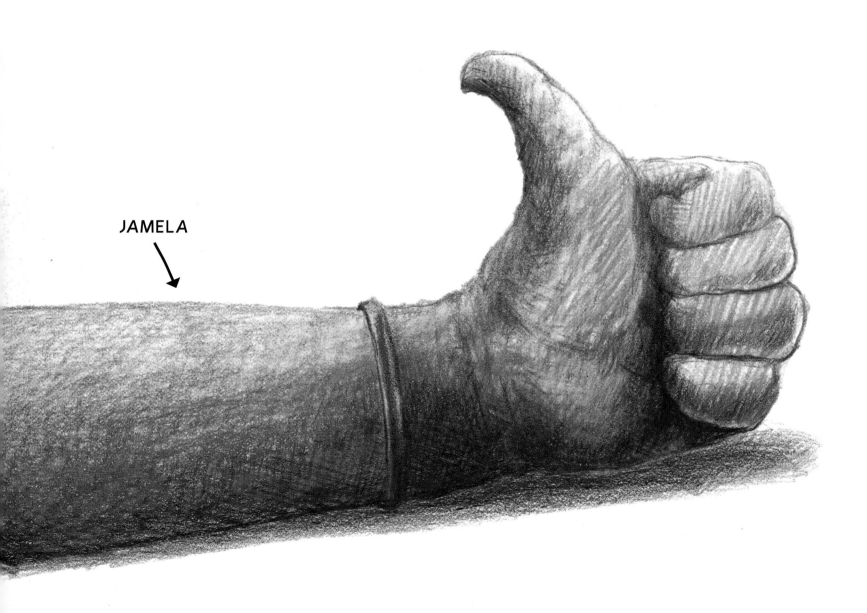

while her cousin Shanice's
thumb is straight.

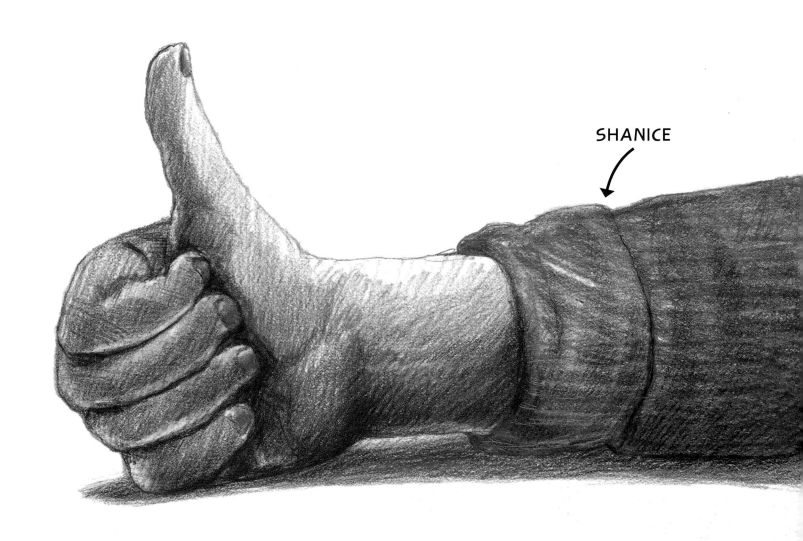

Shanice's second toe is the longest
like her brother, Wayne, her sister, Gilly,

and their second cousins once removed
Gina and Maggie.

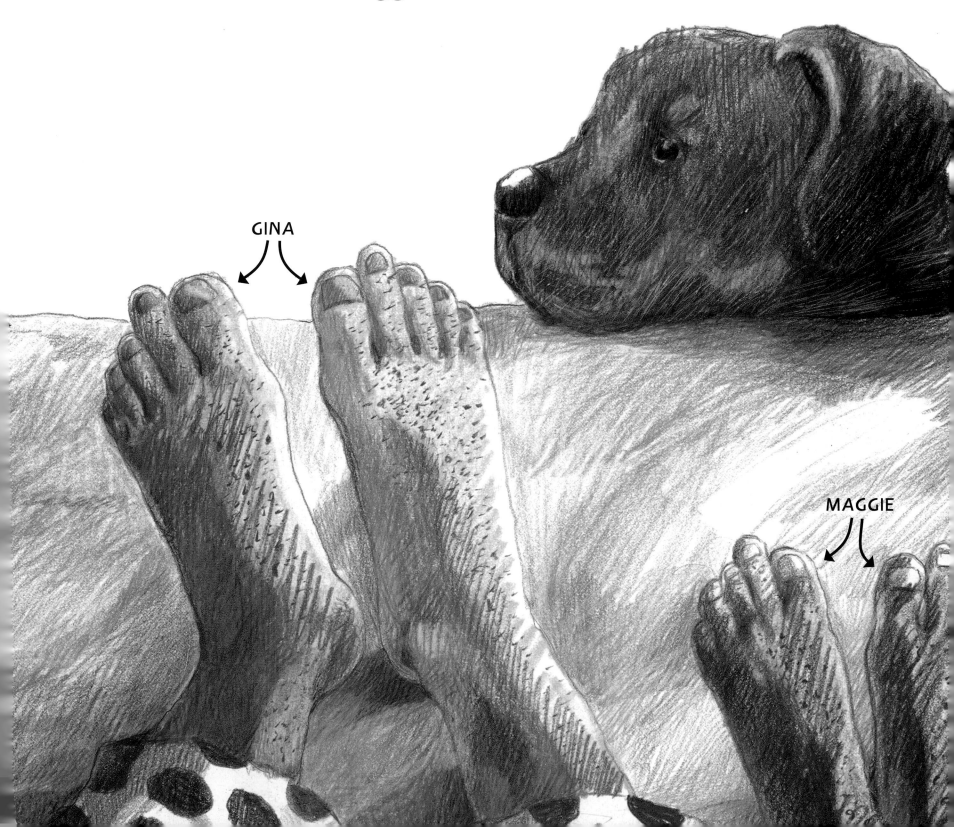

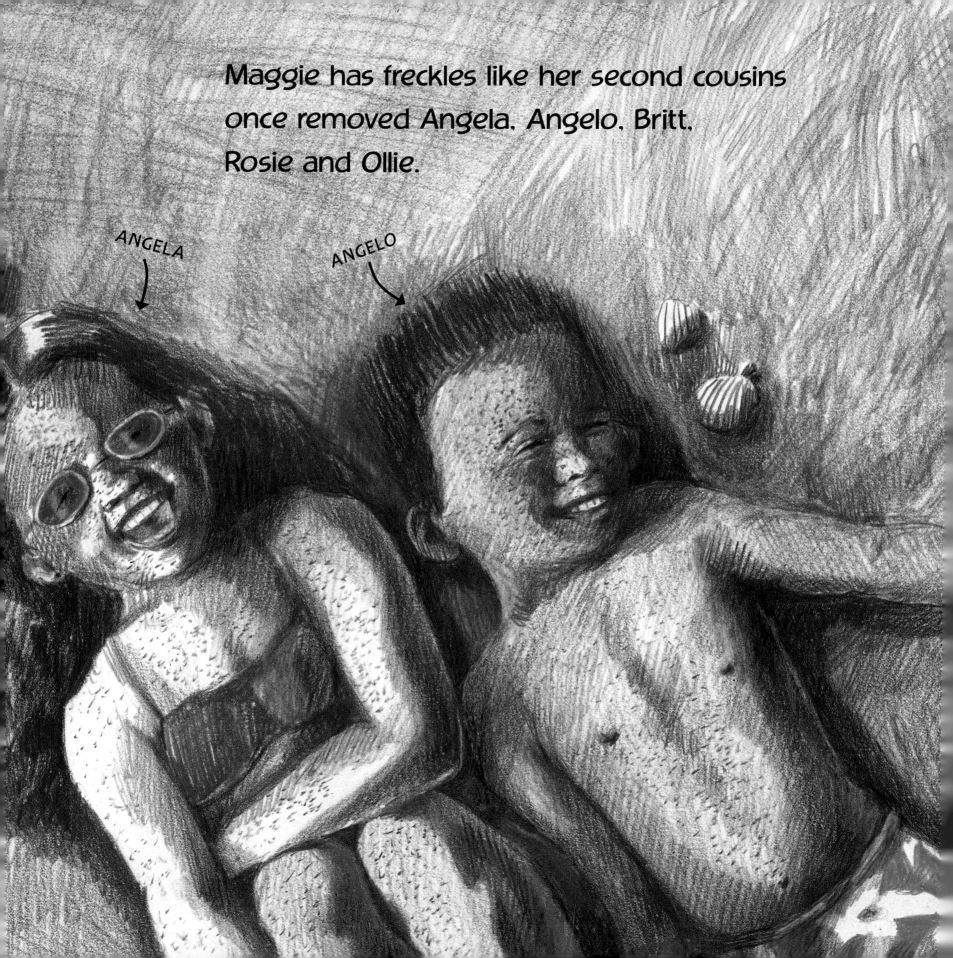

Maggie has freckles like her second cousins once removed Angela, Angelo, Britt, Rosie and Ollie.

Angela, Angelo, Britt, Rosie and Ollie look like their father, Calloway, who has eyebrows

CALLOWAY

that resemble those of his father, Max,
who looks exactly like . . .

MAX

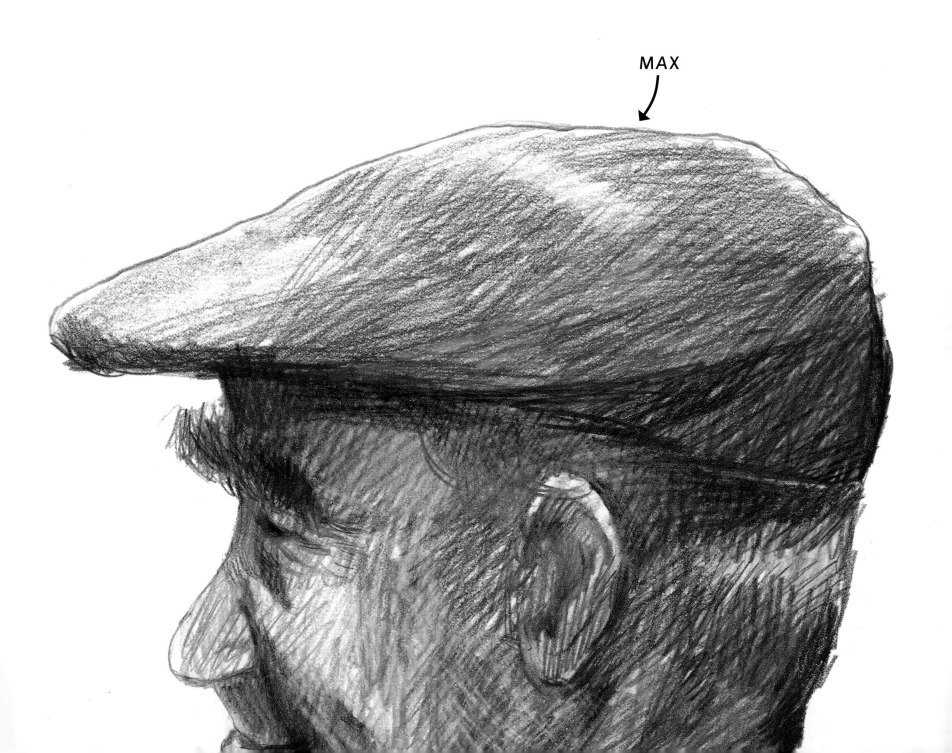

OLLIE

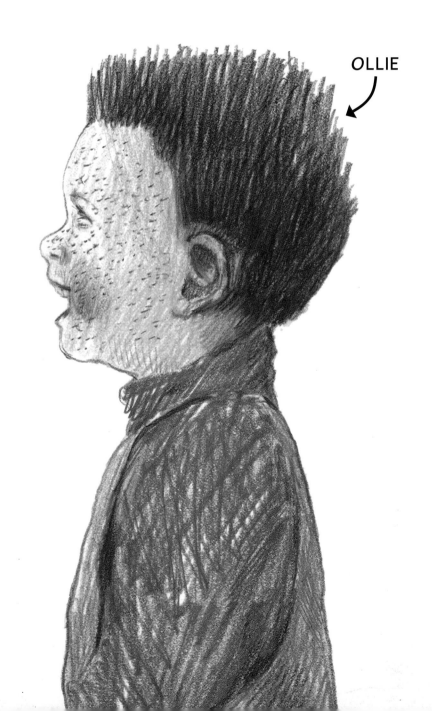

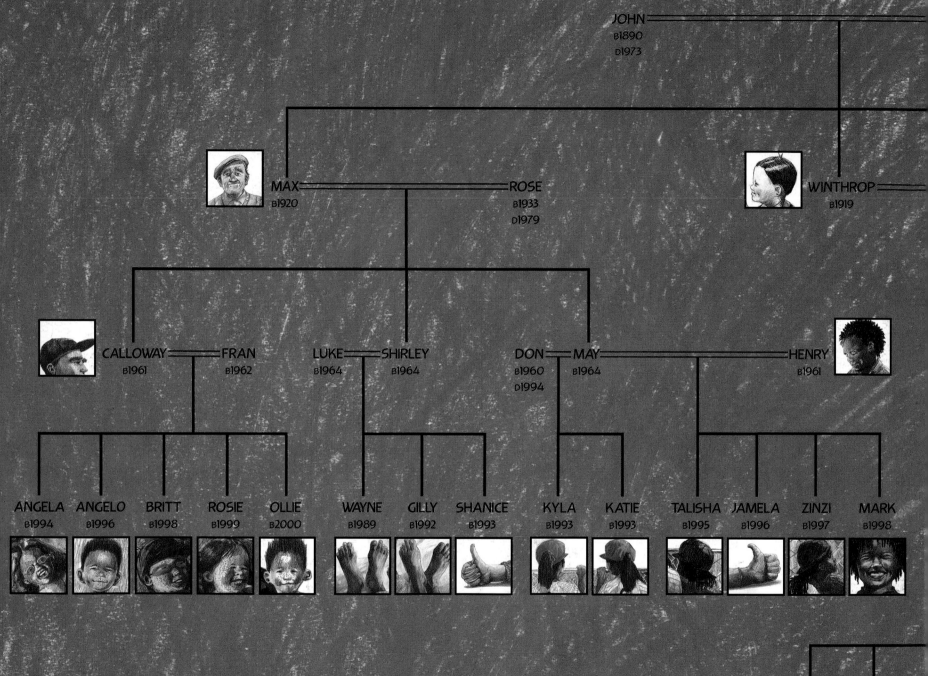

JOHN
B1890
D1973

MAX
B1920

ROSE
B1933
D1979

WINTHROP
B1919

CALLOWAY
B1961

FRAN
B1962

LUKE
B1964

SHIRLEY
B1964

DON
B1960
D1994

MAY
B1964

HENRY
B1961

ANGELA
B1994

ANGELO
B1996

BRITT
B1998

ROSIE
B1999

OLLIE
B2000

WAYNE
B1989

GILLY
B1992

SHANICE
B1993

KYLA
B1993

KATIE
B1993

TALISHA
B1995

JAMELA
B1996

ZINZI
B1997

MARK
B1998

LOUIE
B2001

OLIVIA
B2004